How Will You Leave the World Better Than You Found It?

Written and Illustrated by Urooj Alam Grundmann

ISBN-13: 978-0692625842
ISBN-10: 0692625844

Dedicated to my children, Sofia and Arman. The strength, courage, and wisdom to change the world reside within your heart and mind.

And to my husband, Scott, thank you for your never-ending support. Without your encouragement, I would not dare to dream big.

How will you leave the world
better than you found it?

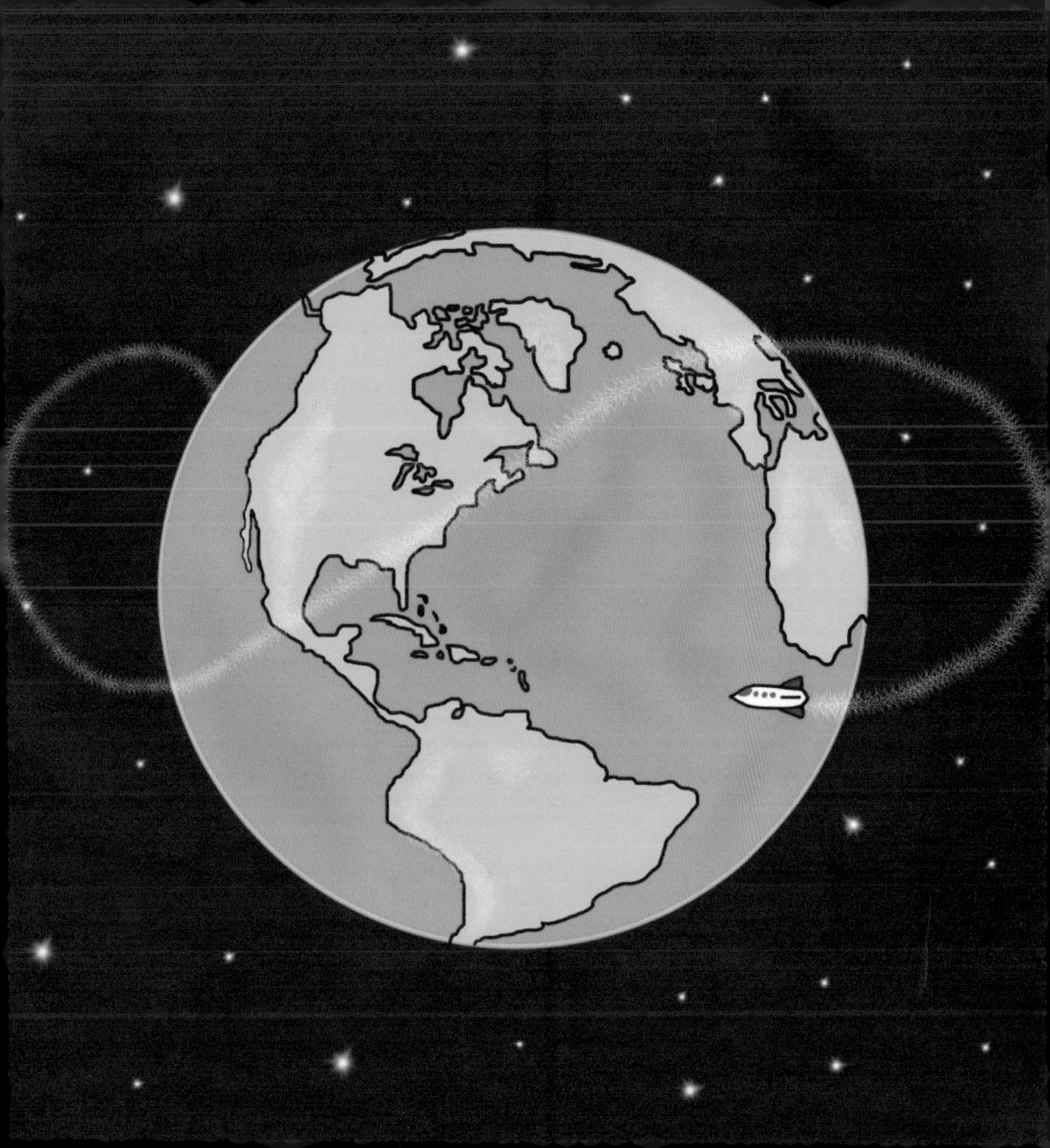

Will you plant a little seed

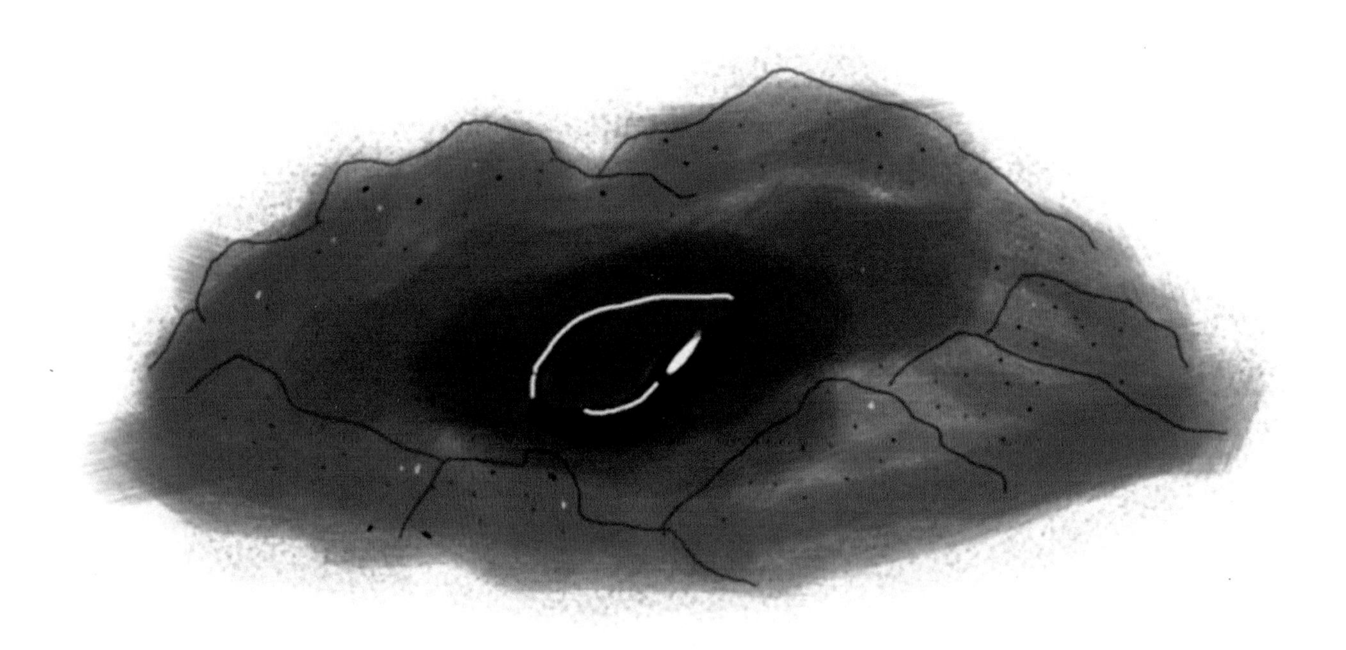

to grow into a great big tree?

Will you volunteer your time
without asking for a dime?

Will you donate your old clothes if you don't really need those?

How about standing up
for what you believe in?

Or always saying "I love you!" whenever you are leaving?

How about teaching someone
how to do what you are good at?

Or giving someone a helping hand, asking,
"Would you like some help with that?"

Will you heal people when they are sick?

Or make them smile with a magic trick?

Will you change laws that are unfair?

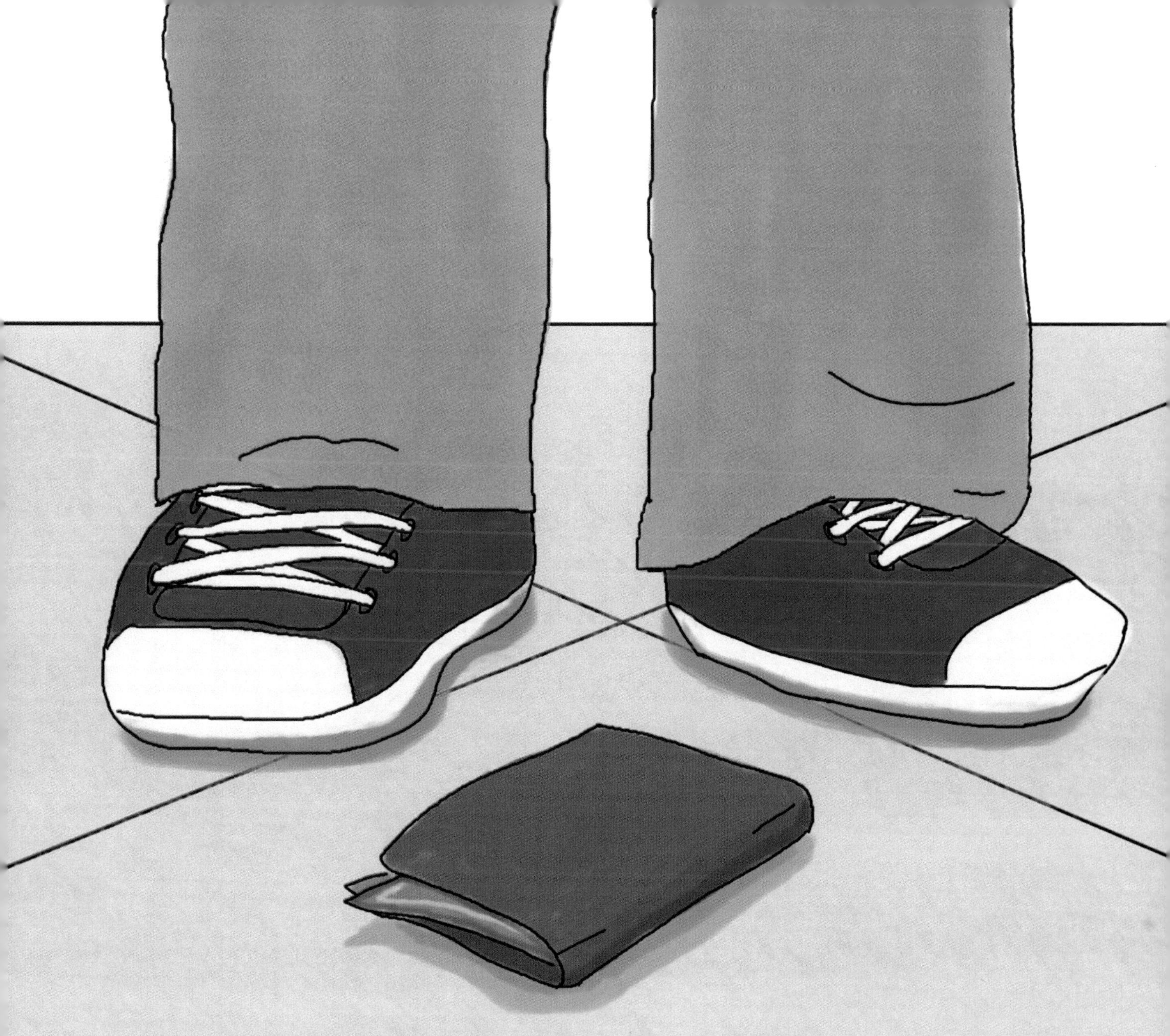

Will you do what's right when no one's there?

Will you be a good friend?

Will you find a heart that you can mend?

Will you keep an open mind
when answers are hard to find?

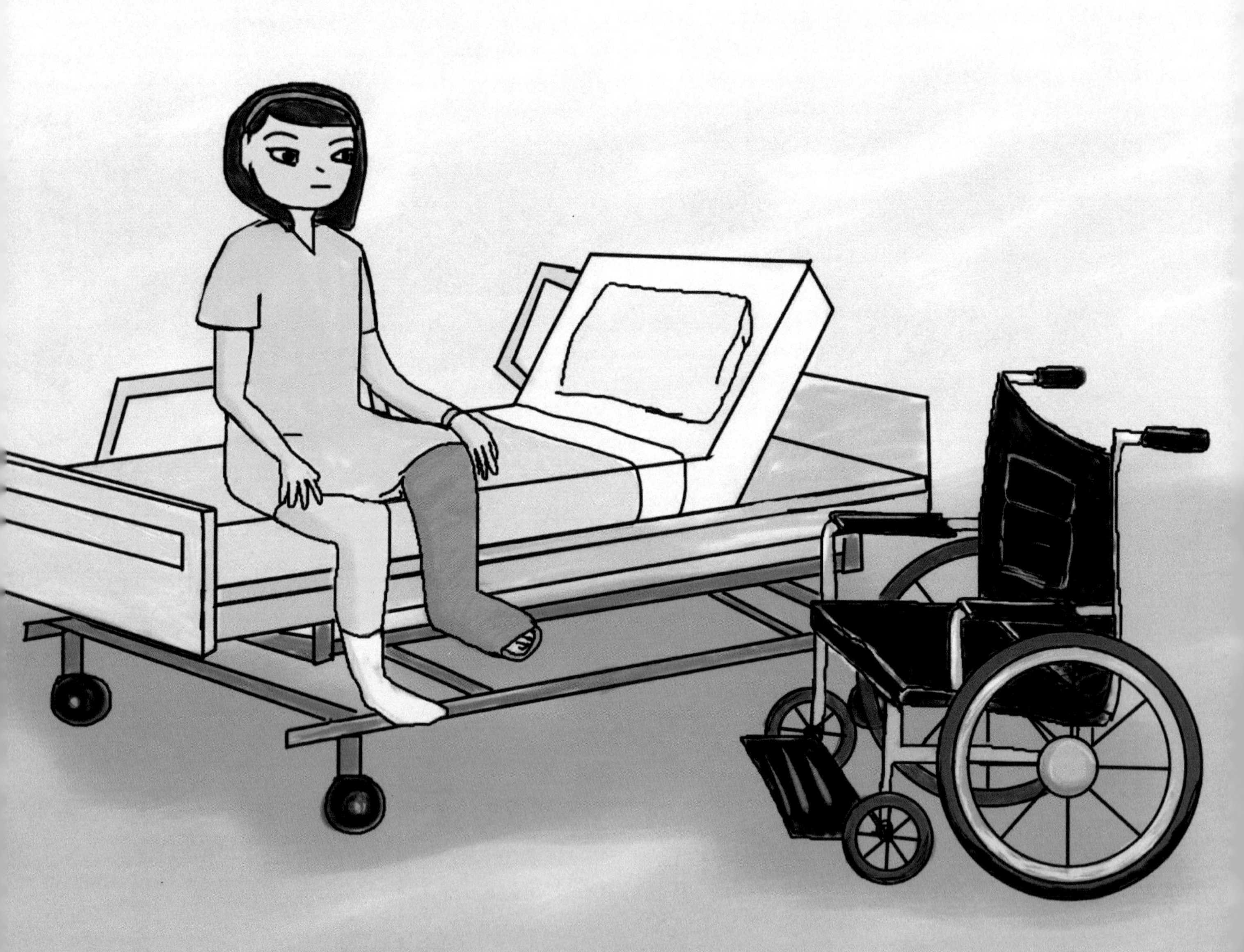

Will you ask a lot of questions?
Will you be open to suggestions?

Will you treat all people

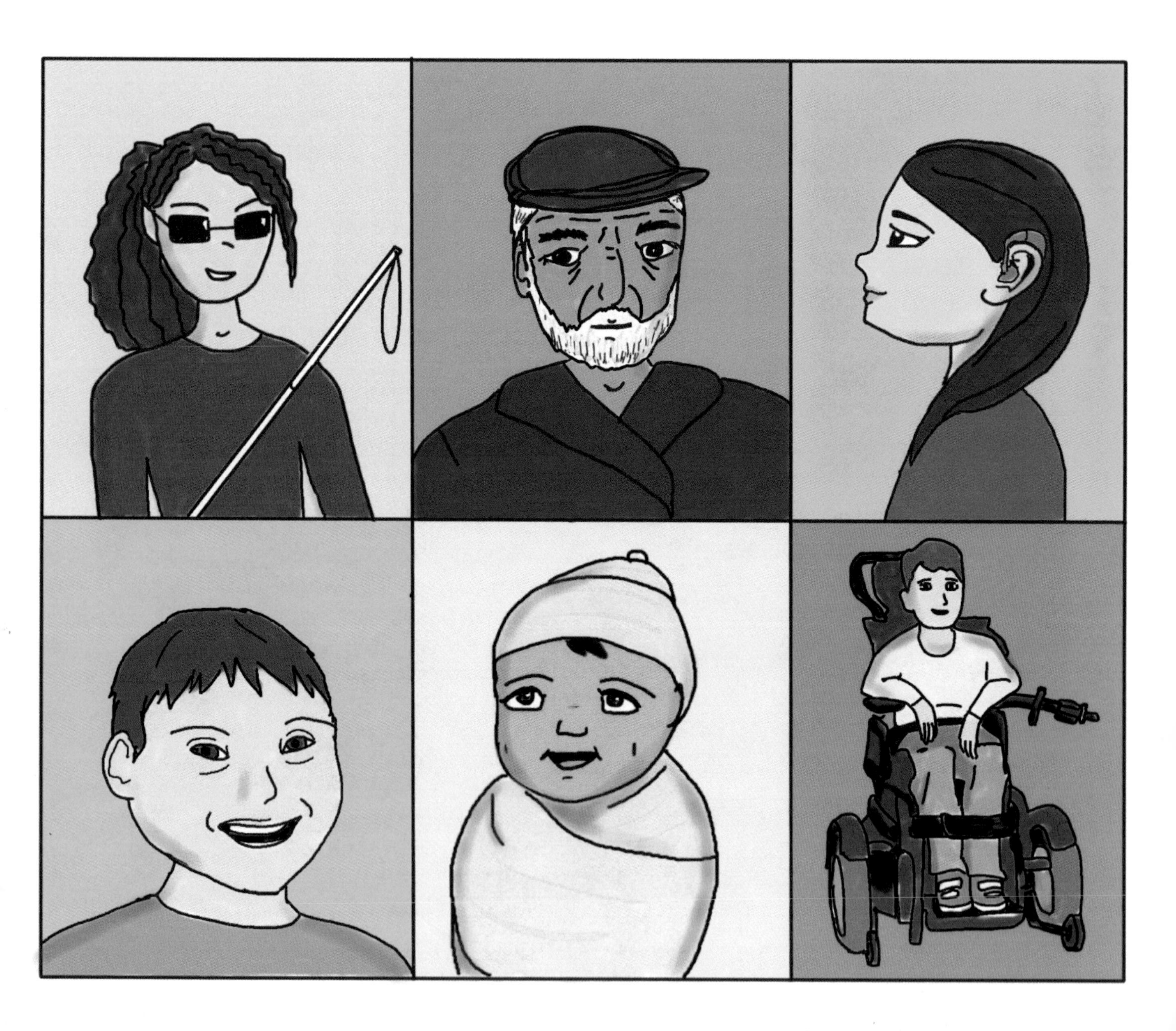

around you as your equal?

Will you help those who are weak?

Will you be the words for those who can't speak?

Will you invent something new?

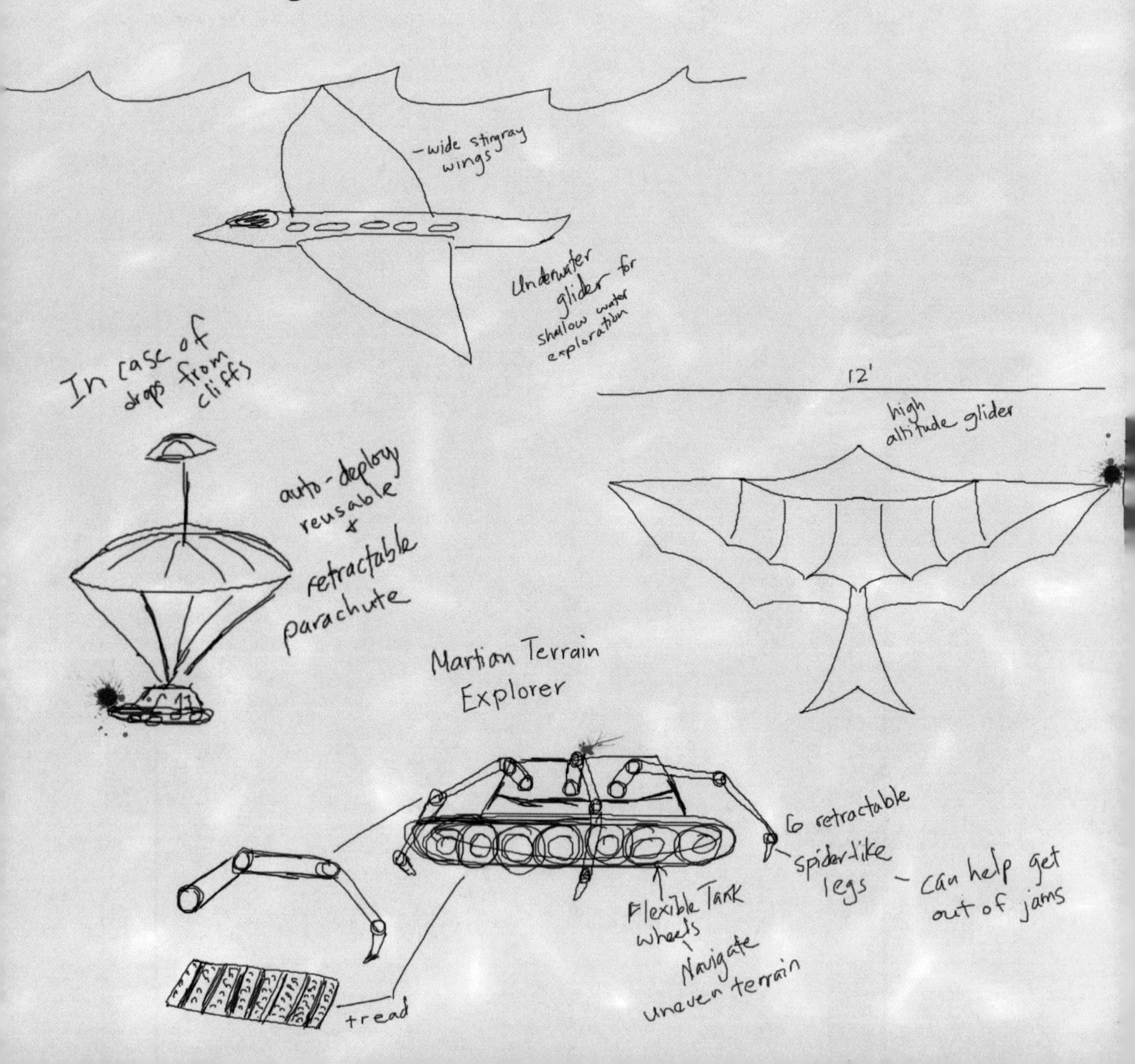

Will you speak words that are true?

Believe in yourself,
whatever you do.

You can change the world

just by being you!

ABOUT THE AUTHOR

Urooj Alam Grundmann is a mother of two and a former elementary school teacher. She enjoys art and writing and has taught 4th grade language arts for five years. Driven by the passion to teach her children how to be positive and productive members of our ever-changing world, she put her ideas and creativity together in her first children's book, *How Will You Leave the World Better Than You Found It?* It is Alam Grundmann's hope that reading this book will inspire people, no matter the age, circumstance, and environment, to think of the impact they can have on making this world a better place for all its inhabitants.

52190365R00019

Made in the USA
Charleston, SC
06 February 2016